The Wishing Well

Brandon Robshaw

Published in association with
The Basic Skills Agency

Acknowledgements
Cover: Dave Smith
Illustrations: Maureen Carter

Orders; please contact Bookpoint Ltd, 39 Milton Park, Abingdon, Oxon OX14
4TD. Telephone: (44) 01235 400414, Fax: (44) 01235 400454. Lines are open
from 9.00–6.00, Monday to Saturday, with a 24 hour message answering service.
Email address: orders@bookpoint.co.uk

British Library Cataloguing in Publication Data
A catalogue record for this title is available from the British Library

ISBN 0 340 77262 X

First published 2000
Impression number 10 9 8 7 6 5 4 3 2 1
Year   2005 2004 2003 2002 2001 2000

Typeset by GreenGate Publishing Services, Tonbridge, Kent.
Printed in Great Britain for Hodder and Stoughton Educational, a division of
Hodder Headline Plc, 338 Euston Road, London NW1 3BH, by Atheneum
Press, Gateshead, Tyne & Wear

The Wishing Well

Contents

1

Nick and Peter

Nick Black hated Peter Moss.
He hated him for being so rich.
He hated him for having such a beautiful wife.
He hated him for having such flash cars,
five of them, in fact.

Nick and Peter were cousins.
They were about the same age.
They had always been rivals as boys.

Peter always had the edge.

He was better at sport.

He did better at school.

He went out with better-looking girls.

It used to drive Nick mad.

Since they had left school,
it was even worse.
Peter had gone into business.
He'd started his own computer
company – and it had made him millions.
Whenever a list was published
of the top hundred business people,
Peter's name was always on it.

Nick, on the other hand, struggled along
with his second-hand car business.
He hardly earned enough to pay the rent.

He wasn't too pleased
when the phone rang one day
and it was Peter.

'I've bought a new house in the country,'
said Peter.
'My dream home.
Ten bedrooms.
Swimming pool, tennis court, the lot.'

'How nice for you,' said Nick.

'Want to come and stay for the weekend?'
asked Peter.

It was the last thing that Nick wanted.
However, he couldn't admit that.
He couldn't let Peter know he was jealous.
'Thanks,' he said. 'I'd love to.'

2

Peter's Dream Home

'Glad you could make it,' said Peter.
'What do you think of the place?'

'Very nice,' said Nick.
The house was old and beautiful.
It was built of grey stone.
It stood in its own grounds.

'My little place in the country,' said Peter.
He laughed.
'Come on in!'

Nick went through into a wood-panelled hall.
There were paintings along the wall.
Nick didn't know anything about paintings.
He was sure these were expensive ones.

At the end of the hall was a large room.
It had the kind of furniture you see
on the Antiques Roadshow.
Peter's wife, Claire, was there.

'Hello, Nick,' she said.
She kissed him on the cheek.
Nick gazed at her.
She really was beautiful.
It wasn't fair.

'Supper will be ready in half an hour,'
said Claire.
'Why don't you guys have a drink
while I see to it?'

That sounded like a good idea to Nick.
He could do with a drink.

'Later,' said Peter.
'I want to show Nick round the grounds.'

'OK,' said Nick, trying to smile.
He followed Peter outside.

'There's the tennis court,' said Peter.
'Great,' said Nick.
Peter also showed him the lake,
the heated swimming pool
and the trees that had been planted
three hundred years ago.

In a little clearing in the trees
stood an old stone well.
'What do you think of that?' said Peter.
'It's older than the house.
They say it's a wishing well.
If you look down it and make a wish,
it will come true.'

'Will it?' asked Nick.

'That's what they say,' said Peter.
'Why don't you try?'

3

The Wishing Well

Nick peered down the well.
'I can't see the bottom,' he said.
'Is there water down there?'

'Oh yes, there's water,' said Peter.
'It's a long way down, though.
Go on, make a wish.'

'Do I have to say it out loud?' said Nick.
He was wondering what to wish for.
'No, just say it to yourself,' Peter told him.

A thought came into Nick's mind.
There was only one thing he really wanted.
He looked down into the darkness of the well.
I wish Peter was dead, he thought.

'Done it?' said Peter.
'I hope it comes true for you.
I think I'll make one too.
I've got everything I want really,
but just for a laugh …'

He leaned over the well.
And suddenly, Nick realised
he could make his wish come true.
It would be easy.
No one would ever know.

Quickly, he grabbed hold of Peter's legs.
'Hey!' said Peter in alarm.
Nick pushed.
Peter fell over the side of the well.
Down, down, down he fell,
screaming all the way.

There was a splash.
Then the sound of Peter's voice calling.
'Help! Help! Help!'
Then more splashing.

Nick waited a few minutes,
until the calling and the splashing
had stopped.
Then he ran back to the house.
'Claire!' he shouted.
'Peter's fallen down the well!
Get a rope!
Quick, before it's too late!'

But of course, it was too late.

4

Nick and Claire

The police questioned Nick.
He could tell they suspected him,
but Nick stuck to his story.
Peter had lost his balance and fallen in.
The police might not have believed it.
However, they couldn't prove a thing.

Claire didn't suspect him at all.
She thought he'd tried to save Peter.
She saw a lot of Nick.
He helped her to arrange the funeral.

During the service, he sat next to her.
When she cried, he put his arm around her.

After the funeral,
Nick met Claire quite often.
He went round to the house.
She was glad to see him. She needed company.

One night, after he had stayed for supper,
he leaned over the table and kissed her.
Claire held him tightly.
'I've been so lonely,' she said.

'You don't need to be lonely any more,'
Nick told her.
He kissed her again.

'You don't think that –
Peter would mind, do you?'
asked Claire.

'It's just what he would have wanted,'
said Nick.
On his way home,
he stopped at the wishing well
and made a wish.

His wish came true.
A month later, he and Claire were married.

Nick felt pretty pleased with himself.
He'd got rid of Peter.
Now he had Peter's beautiful wife
and beautiful house for himself.
He'd got what he wanted out of life.
Nothing could spoil it for him now.

5

Baby Ella

A year after their marriage,
Claire gave birth to a baby daughter.
They called her Ella.

Nick loved being a father.
He spent a lot of time with Ella.
He didn't work now –
he had sold Peter's business.
He lived a life of comfort and ease.

He was happy now.
He felt that he had become
a much nicer person.
It was funny that he'd had to kill a man
to become nicer.
But Nick tried not to think about that.

Ella was a bright girl.
She was talking by the time she was one.
She loved nursery rhymes and songs.
When friends came round,
Nick always asked Ella to sing to them.

One day, Nick got a nasty shock.
Some friends had come over for lunch.
'Sing us a song, Ella!' said Nick.

Ella opened her mouth wide.
She sang in her loudest voice:
'Ding dong bell!
Peter's in the well!'

The guests laughed, then stopped.
Claire looked upset.
Nick couldn't speak.

'Who put him in?' sang Ella.

'That's enough!' shouted Nick.
'Sing something else!'

Ella looked at her Dad,
surprised by his angry voice.
She started to cry.

Nick walked out of the room.
He went and sat on the terrace.
He was trembling.

It didn't mean anything, he told himself.
Ella got the words of the song wrong –
so what?
Kids were always getting the words
of things wrong.

But he still felt uneasy.
Far away, among the trees,
he could just see the old stone wishing well.
Of course, Peter wasn't in it any more.
He'd been buried.

But what if his ghost
was haunting the spot?
What if his ghost
was putting words into Ella's mouth?

Nick didn't sleep well that night.

6

Bad Dreams

Soon after this,
Nick began to have bad dreams.
He kept dreaming that Peter
was climbing out of the well.
Creeping through the grounds towards him,
dripping with water.

His dead, dripping face
stared in through the window.

'Ella should have been my daughter,'
he said.
'I want her.
Let me take her.'

'No! No!' screamed Nick.
He woke up in terror.
Claire was shaking him.

'Calm down,' she said.
'It was another bad dream.
It's all right now.'

Nick wiped the sweat from his face.
'No one will take Ella from us,
will they?' he asked.
'She's safe with us, isn't she?'

'Of course she's safe with us,'
said Claire.

This was Nick's greatest fear –
that somehow, Ella would be snatched away.

He watched Ella every minute of the day.
It wasn't easy to keep an eye on her.
She was walking now
and she loved wandering off.
She liked squeezing into little corners –
under the stairs, or behind an armchair –
to hide.

Nick always made sure
he knew where she was.
He told Claire to watch her at all times, too.

Claire thought he was making
a bit of a fuss –
of course she'd keep an eye on Ella.
But what was all the worry about?
They were in their own house, weren't they?
Ella wasn't going to disappear.

But Claire was wrong.
One summer evening,
without any warning,
Ella disappeared.

7

Ella Goes Missing

Nick was sitting on the terrace,
enjoying the evening sunshine.
Pigeons were cooing.
Ella, he knew, was in the kitchen with Claire.
All his fears seemed unreal now.
There was nothing to worry about.

Claire came out with a drink for him.
'Here you are, darling.'

'Thanks,' said Nick.
'But you shouldn't leave Ella
on her own, you know.
What's she doing?'

'I didn't leave her,' said Claire.
'I thought she was with you.'

There was a short silence.
Then Nick jumped from his chair.
'What?' he shouted.
'You mean you don't know where she is?'

'Calm down,' said Claire.
'She can't have gone far.'
But she was worried too.

'Go and check in the house!'
said Nick.
'I'll try the grounds!'

Claire hurried back inside.
Nick ran through the grounds.
'Ella!' he called. 'Ella!'
There was no answer.

Ahead of him, he saw the wishing well.
A horrible thought came to him.
What if poor Ella had wandered off to the well
and fallen in it?

He ran towards it.

8

The Last Wish

As he got close,
he calmed down.
The wall of the well was much too high
for Ella to climb.
That was plain to see.
But where was she?

Then Nick had another thought.
The last two wishes he had made
at this wishing well had come true.
He would try a third.

He leaned over the edge of the well
and peered down
into the blackness.
I wish that Ella is OK, he thought.

A moment later, he heard a shout
from the house.
It was Claire.
'It's all right!
I've found her!
Relief flooded through Nick.
Thank God, he thought.
Oh, thank God.
He leaned on the edge of the well,
getting his breath back.

Down in the darkness,
something seemed to be moving.
Nick watched it,
not understanding.
The moving thing got closer.
Nick made to step back.

But the moving thing was too quick.
Two thin, slimy arms reached up
and grabbed him by the neck.
Nick found himself staring
into a blurred, drowned face.

'My wish came true,' said the face.
'The last wish I ever made.
I had to wait a long time,
but it's come true.
I'm so glad it's come true.'

The grip tightened on Nick's neck.
He struggled furiously.
But the grip was too strong.
Suddenly, Nick lost his footing.
He tumbled over the edge
and fell into the well.

And Peter held him tight
all the way down.